'FOR THERE HAD
ONCE BEEN
FALSE IDOLS
AND ASSES' HEADS
DRAWN ON
THE WALLS...'

DANILO KIŠ
Born 1935, Subotica, Yugoslavia
Died 1989, Paris, France

'The Legend of the Sleepers' and 'Simon Magus' published in
The Encyclopedia of the Dead, 1983.

KIŠ IN PENGUIN MODERN CLASSICS
The Encyclopedia of the Dead

DANILO KIŠ

The Legend of the Sleepers

Translated by Michael Henry Heim

Revised by Mark Thompson

PENGUIN BOOKS

PENGUIN CLASSICS

UK | USA | Canada | Ireland | Australia
India | New Zealand | South Africa

Penguin Books is part of the Penguin Random House group
of companies whose addresses can be found at
global.penguinrandomhouse.com.

This selection first published 2018
001

Copyright © Danilo Kiš and Globus, 1983

Translation copyright © Farrar, Straus and Giroux, 1989

Set in 10.25/12.75 pt Dante MT Std
Typeset by Jouve (UK), Milton Keynes
Printed in Great Britain by Clays Ltd, St Ives plc

ISBN: 978-0-241-33937-4

www.greenpenguin.co.uk

Contents

The Legend of the Sleepers

They stayed in their cave three hundred years, increased by nine.

KORAN, XVIII: 25

I

They lay on their backs on rough, damp haircloth that was somewhat mildewed from the humidity and had worn through in places from their movements, their twitching, their bones wherever their bodies were in contact with the camel hair – at the back of the head, at shoulder blades and elbows, near a protruding pelvis, beneath heels and calves rigid as distaffs.

They lay on their backs, with their hands crossed in prayer like corpses, on damp and rotting haircloth that had worn thin beneath their bodies from the rare unconscious twitching of weary sleepers, sleepers weary of life and movement but sleepers nonetheless; for their limbs did move, though imperceptibly to the human eye, and the haircloth beneath them had worn thin in places where it had been pressed against the rock of the cave by the weight of their sleep and their stone-like bodies, where it had been exposed to the stirring of human clay, the chafing of bones on the dank haircloth, and the hair-cloth rubbing on the diamantine rock of the cave.

They lay on their backs in the tranquil repose of great sleep-ers, but the movements of their limbs in the darkness of time wore thin the wet haircloth beneath them, gnawing at the fibers of the camel hair, which were abraded imperceptibly, as when water, coupled with time, begins to bore into the hard heart of stone.

They lay on their backs in a dark cave on Mount Celius, with their hands crossed in prayer like corpses, all three of them, Dionysius and his friend Malchus and, a short distance away, John, the saintly shepherd, and his dog, Qitmir.

Beneath their eyelids burdened by sleep, their eyelids anointed with the balsam and hemlock of sleep, the greenish crescents of their dead eyes did not show through, for the darkness was too profound, the dank darkness of time, the murk of the cave of eternity.

From the walls and vaults of the cave, eternal water dripped drop by drop and flowed in a barely audible murmur through the veins of the rocks like the blood in the veins of the sleep-ers, and from time to time a drop fell on their torpid bodies, on their stone-like faces, and ran down the wrinkles in their foreheads into the shell of an ear, lingered in the curved wrin-kles of an eyelid, trickled across a greenish eyeball like an icy tear, or halted on the lashes of a petrified eye. Yet they did not awaken.

Deaf, their ears plugged by the lead of sleep and the pitch of darkness, they lay motionless, staring into the darkness of their beings, the darkness of time and eternity, which had turned their sleeping hearts to stone, which had halted their breath and the movement of their lungs, which had frozen the murmur of blood in their veins.

The only thing that grew – nourished by the moisture of the cave and the immobility of the bodies, stimulated by the ashes of oblivion and the frenzy of dreams – was the hair on their heads and the stubble on their faces, the fuzz on their bodies and the fuzz under their arms; the only thing that grew in their sleep – invisibly, as water builds and destroys invisibly – were their nails, crackling.

2

The youngest, Dionysius, who had a rose at his heart and who lay between his friend Malchus and John the shepherd, was the first to wake, suddenly, as if touched by the wind of time and memory. The first thing he heard was the dripping of water from the vaults of the cave; the first thing he felt was a thorn in his heart. Immersed in silence, his consciousness, a weary sleeper's consciousness steeped in the dank darkness of the cave, was unable to collect itself at once, for his body was torpid from long repose and his soul was clouded by dreams.

In his soul he calls out the name of the Lord his God, calls out the sweet name of his Prisca, and remembers everything that happened, recalled it with the horror of a man dying and the joy of a man in love. For what happened to his soul and his body – he no longer knows when – seemed once more like

3

a dream; perhaps it was no more than a dream now, a nightmare of life and a nightmare of death, a nightmare of unrequited love, a nightmare of time and eternity.

To the left and right he felt the bodies of his friend Malchus and John the shepherd smitten with a dead sleep; he felt them even though they slept without breath or movement, as mute as mummies, lacking even the odor of human bodies, the smell of human decay; he felt the presence of their disembodied essence, sensed, somewhere to the right, near John's legs, the disembodied, mummified body of the shepherd's dog, its front paws extended, lying at its master's side and keeping a life-and-death watch over his dead sleep.

3

His stone-like body, his torpid limbs still stretched out on the frayed haircloth whose moisture he did not feel, Dionysius painfully separates the fingers of his crossed hands, fingers so stiff from sleep and immobility that they seemed to have grown together, and he remembers his body and his bodily existence, remembers his heart, which – lo! – has come alive in him, as had his innards and his lungs and his eyes sealed by the lead of sleep and his member, cold and sleeping, as distant as sin was distant from him.

And he returns his consciousness to the heart of the cave, to its clotted pitch-black darkness, and listens for the eternal clepsydra of time, for he wished his bodiless being to inhabit time, his consciousness and his body to inhabit the heart of time once again, and return to the time before this dream and this cave. And first he remembers Prisca's sweet name, for she had been in his dreams and his reality, in his own heart and the heart of time, in the heart of sleep and the heart of waking.

At first he did not know what to do, as he did not wish to awaken his weary, somnolent companions, his accomplices in dreams, and he plunged with his own consciousness into the river of time to separate dream from reality, to grasp – with the aid of his consciousness and his memories, with the aid of his Lord God to whom he prayed – what had happened.

Yet there was nothing in him but memories of his own dream and his awakening, what had been and what was now; there was still nothing in him but the indissoluble darkness prevailing before the Creation, before Genesis, when the Lord had not yet divided light from darkness and day from night, when the Lord had not yet distinguished dream from reality and reality from dream.

And had it not been for the rose at his heart, the sweet name of Prisca, her memory etched in his body, her presence in his heart, his skin, his consciousness, his empty innards, he would not have awoken at all.

4

For she was no longer the Prisca of old, the Prisca of his bygone dreams, the Prisca he had found at the gates of his recent sleep, in the heart of his recent awakening. Alas, she was no longer the Prisca unto whom he had made eternal vows, no longer his Prisca of earlier dreams and an earlier reality; she was not – God forgive him – the same woman, the daughter of Emperor Decius, enemy of Christianity, or the same dream of the same woman; she was not his Prisca, who had pledged herself to him for all eternity; she was another woman with Prisca's name and very like her yet not the same Prisca, similar to her in shape, but no, not she.

And he conjured up the living, all too painfully living memory of her image, the image of his Prisca, but now it was the image of two women merged by time and memory into one, without limits or bounds, for they were made of the dust and ashes of two memories, the clay of two successive creations into which sleep had breathed a soul, his soul.

And the two images solidified in his consciousness, his memory, and he kneaded the clay of which they were made, and in the end he could no longer distinguish two women, two dreams, but only one, Prisca of the almond eyes, his Prisca, present and past, and the memory fills him with joy and strength, enough to wrest him from sleep yet not enough to move his torpid limbs, for he is overcome with fear of his own thoughts at the very moment that he winds up the thread of remembrance and remembers everything that happened before this sleep.

5

And he sees the light of the torches, which shine down like stars from the vault of the cave above their heads, and he remembers and hears the murmur of the throng that gathered around them and then the silence that reigned for a moment and the shout and flight of the crowd when John, the saintly shepherd, raises his arms to heaven and calls out the name of the Lord.

Was it a dream? Was it the dream of a sleepwalker, a dream within a dream, and hence more real than a real dream, since it cannot be measured against waking, since it cannot be measured by consciousness, because it is a dream from which one awakens into another dream? Or was it a god-like dream, a dream of time and eternity? A dream without illusions and doubts, a dream with its own language and senses, a dream of both soul and body, a dream of consciousness and corporality both, a dream with clear-cut boundaries, with its own language and sound, a dream that is palpable, that can be explored with taste, smell, and hearing, a dream stronger than waking, a dream such as only the dead perhaps can dream, a dream that cannot be denied by a razor nicking your chin, for blood flows at once, and everything you do is further proof of reality and waking; skin and heart bleed alike in the dream, the body rejoices in the dream as does the soul, the only miracle in this dream is life itself; awakening from this dream means awakening into death.

They had no time even for leave-taking, for each of them was absorbed in his soul and his forgiveness, and each to himself and then all in unison they began whispering prayers with their dry lips, for they knew the throng would return and had left only to summon Decius's legionaries or prepare the cages of wild animals, putting guards at the entrance of the cave until all is ready for their slaughter, which the populace, the godless multitude, will relish.

6

And they came again bearing torches and lanterns that illumined the cave with a new and powerful light, came chanting songs and psalms, and with children bearing candles and icons, and the cave was illumined with their pious song and prayers, the voices of the priests resounding among the rocks, the voices of the children, all boys in white, like a choir of heavenly hosts.

Before long, the cave fills with the smoke of torches and the fragrance of incense, and everyone sang the glory of the Lord in a loud voice; the priests and the children and the three of them, Dionysius, Malchus, and John, the saintly shepherd, they all sang psalms to the glory of Jesus the Nazarene, the miracle worker and redeemer.

Was that, too, a dream? Was it a vision, or were they at the heavenly gates? Was it the end of a nightmare and dream, or was it their ascension to heaven?

He gazed on them with a troubled soul, as those in the gallery gazed upon the three men. And in the light of the torches he sees their faces and their raiment, and he was greatly surprised to find that they were scarlet and crimson, made of sheepskin dyed red, trimmed in gold and silver and bronze. And before them they held icons gleaming with gold and silver and precious stones.

8

7

Then several muscular young men stand forward from the crowd, bow before them, and, after making the sign of the cross and kissing their hands and feet, lift them one by one, as effortlessly as if they were children, and carry them across the cave's rocky floor, holding them carefully, like icons, barely touching them with their powerful hands, while the crowd lit their steps and their way, still singing to the glory of the Lord.

At the head of the procession they carried John, the saintly shepherd, his hands clasped in prayer, whispering his simple prayer, which God prefers to all others; next they carried Malchus, who had a long, white beard and was arrayed, like John, in bright robes embroidered with gold; and last, rocking slightly in the powerful arms of his bearers as in a boat, came Dionysius.

Was that, too, a dream?

And he sees the shaved heads of the young men on whose shoulders the litter conveying his body rested, a body he too felt was as light as that of a child or a feeble old man. This ascension – was it, too, a dream? And this singing and the eyes of the young men carrying him, who dared not gaze up at him, so that all he saw were thick eyebrows beneath low foreheads and lashes below half-shut lids; the bare, powerful necks and, lit by a ray of light, the crowns of the heads of those carrying Malchus before him as they mounted a slope, moving closer to the sky and the heavenly paradise, while the crowd standing on either side of them lifted torches and lanterns high above their heads, and he, not daring to look them in the eye, not even for an instant, lest he find beneath the half-shut lids the vacant, greenish eyeballs of insensible sleepwalkers who wander in their sleep and chant psalms and prayers, who in their deep slumber, their wandering slumber, carry the three of them past the cave's stone whirlpools, down deep gorges and up slippery cliffs, across vast, capacious halls and temples of crystal foam, through narrow passageways beneath low vaults.

And whence their sure step, the sublime composure with which they skirt all dangers, carrying their load with skill and grace, barely touching it with their powerful hands?

In vain did he try to dispel his doubts, to find a gaze, a human eye in which to glimpse his face, in which to discover his image, proof that he was awake. If only he can catch the eye of a child, one of the angels in white robes standing above him on either side of the path, to both left and right, in the crystal gallery, as in a temple – but in vain. No sooner does he think one of the children was glancing at him with its angelic, human eyes, no sooner does he think one of them sought his glance, no sooner does he turn his eyes in its direction than it turns its gaze away, lowering the curtain of its leaden lids and opaque lashes while continuing to sing its song and, eyes now tightly shut, to open its round mouth like a fish, and he, Dionysius, feels a certain hypocrisy in that hidden glance, that fish-like mouth, a deliberate withholding, a fear or respect, or the torpor of a sleepwalker.

For only sleepwalkers can move as they moved, sleepwalkers led over the abyss by a sovereign hand, by the daring of people who do not see the deep chasm beneath their feet and the madness of people sustained by the power of their ancient divinity, the pagan power of bodies that still recall the faith of ancestors who bowed down to the moon, their procession and their outstretched arms a tribute to Luna, pagan goddess of the moon, whence the souls of their departed call down to them, for that procession is merely the call of blood and the call of time. And he dared not utter a word, lest he should awaken the slumbering pagans, the sleepwalkers, who had gathered in the cave to celebrate their festival, to honor their pagan goddess – for surely a full moon is shining outside.

8

And he dared not utter a word save the prayer he whispered to himself, scarcely moving his lips, for he feared he would awaken from his sleepwalking enchantment and send them all toppling into the murky depths over which they now bore him, treading barefoot and all but soundlessly through the dank cave, which sparkled with glistening drops; his voice and his awakening would have drawn them all back into the murky chasm out of which the sleepwalkers are now carrying them, up the slope, higher and higher, and in their fear of awakening they would all have toppled into the abyss yawning below them, deep into the dark bowels of the cave, which not even the light of the torches can reach but whose depths and precipices are present in his waking, sleepwalking consciousness. And he hears a stone fall beneath the bare feet of those carrying him, hears it tumbling down, skipping from rock to rock, fleet and resonant, then more hesitant and hushed, retreating like an echo, but the sound never ceased, it merely faded, for it did not touch bottom any more than did his half-wakeful, half-dormant consciousness.

Is it a dream or a sleepwalking illusion of his half-dormant consciousness, a dream of his pagan body, descending as it did from pagan ancestors, worshippers of the moon goddess, the full-moon goddess, ancestors who are calling to him now? Surely there is a full moon outside or a new moon at least, and the souls of his ancestors are awakening, the souls of his ancient forebears, calling to his pagan body, tempting his pagan blood.

Or is it the ascension of his soul to heaven, the moment when soul shears away from body, Christian soul from pagan body, sinful body from sinful soul, to which mercy is granted, whose sins are forgiven?

Are they a dream, the dog carried next to John, cradled like the Lamb of God, and the boy pressing the dog Qitmir to his bosom like a sacrificial lamb or pagan idol and carrying it over gorges and ravines, clasping it to his heart like the Good Shepherd, his eyes pinned to the ground, venturing not so much as a glance into Qitmir's cloudy green-blue eyes veiled by the cataracts of sleep, eyes green and blue like plums, eyes half open, all but extinguished and blind. Nor does he, Dionysius, dare catch Qitmir's eye now that the boy with the dog has paused at his side to let the litter bearers, hugging the ground and virtually on all fours, through the narrow passage; and he, Dionysius, feels as though he were hovering above the rocks, always in the same position, half-reclining, his head slightly raised and resting on the chest of one of his bearers; and he hears only the bearers' quiet, restrained breathing. The boy and the dog have disappeared, for the boy paused before the narrow neck of the cave to let through the men who are carrying the three of them, that is, John, Malchus, and himself, Dionysius; the boy, his eyes pinned to the ground, remained behind at the entrance to the narrow cleft in the cave to wait his turn, still clutching the blue-eyed Qitmir in his arms.

9

Light flickered in from both ends of the narrow passageway, behind him barely visible, ahead of him, at the end of the tunnel, brighter and brighter, filtering through the sharp teeth of Polyphemus's massive, gaping jaws, for such it clearly was: the entry to the cave of long ago, and he remembers it now as he remembers the story John the saintly shepherd told him then, in that first dream or first reality. The passageway has been widened, or so it seems to him, and he could see from the shoulders of his bearers that the wall of the cave had been smoothed over at this point, he could see the gaping jaw and its broken eyeteeth, shiny, even, white and crystalline at the tip, with fresh diagonal notches, absolutely white and as dazzling as salt, on short rust-colored stumps.

Was that, too, a dream?

And the cripples who started swarming about their feet, wriggling like worms, kissing their hands and feet even before their strong bearers managed to carry them out of the cave. And the entrance to the cave, which he remembered well for its desecrated vaults and the drawings that shepherds had scratched into the hard stone with rocks or knives – for there had once been false idols and asses' heads drawn on the walls by the sinful hands of shepherds, and, as high as the human hand could reach, lewd figures, and there had been the stench of human excrement.

And now – lo! – the lewd figures and asses' heads have been erased, though fresh traces of scraping and filing are still visible on the rock, and the smell of human excrement has evaporated, they must have cleaned it up; there are now lanterns and fragrant torches hanging from chinks in the walls of the cave, the vault is covered with flowers and laurel wreaths and icons inlaid with gold, and the floor is spread with a carpet of flowers, now trampled by the bare feet of the litter bearers while the people sing psalms and whisper prayers.

The blind and the crippled, wriggling like worms, swarm about his feet, kissing his body and begging in words muffled and horrible, begging him in the name of love and faith, the sun and the moon, life and death, heaven and hell, begging and imploring him to restore their sight, heal their wounds and deadened limbs, restore the light of day and the light of faith.

Are they a dream or a nightmare, the cripples begging for alms, the poor wretches who beat one another with their crutches and scratch one another's eyes out for the mercy of his body, for the mercy of being healed – is this a dream? His impotence to utter a word to them, to do a thing for them, these poor wretches, these cripples whom the muscular young men remove from the path of the procession, pushing them aside, blind and frail, lame and paralyzed – is this a dream? His impotence to grasp it all, the miracle, the suffering, his own impotence, his helplessness to do anything for the wretches who beg and plead with him, to tell them of his helplessness, to ask for *their* mercy, for a human word, to implore them to believe him, believe in his impotence, to win them over with curses and entreaties so that they can tell him what is happening to him, whether it is all a dream, those dead, blind eyes turning to him, vacant and gruesome, rolling, bloody and gruesome, those blind eyes seeking him out and finding him, for they are the only eyes he saw, the only eyes that turned to him, that took pity and turned to him, for not even the cripples who drag themselves up to him on their stumps to kiss his feet with their icy lips, not even they granted him a glance, they too embrace him and plead with him without looking at him, raising only their mutilated arms in a half embrace and clasping their stumps in a gruesome half prayer that ends at the elbows – in the misshapen wrinkles and seams of mutilated half limbs.

Is it a nightmare, is it his ascension to heaven? Is it a nightmare of the purgatory through which his body must pass, is it the final punishment, the final admonition to a sinful body, that spectacle of human horror which serves the soul, before its ascension, by reminding it of hell?

Is it a nightmare or perhaps only the Calvary of his body and soul, hell itself where they are taking his body to be roasted and quartered, and the prayers, the heavenly singing, the light and the procession by shoulder, on the wings of angels, were these nothing but the last temptation of a sinful soul so the soul will recall paradise lost, the gardens of paradise and delights of paradise of which it is not worthy, the Lord bearing him past these gardens on the wings of fallen angels that his soul might experience rapture and bliss, experience the fragrance of incense and myrrh, the balm of prayer, in order to suffer the torments of hell more acutely, for prayers and hymns will ring in the soul's memory, the fragrances of fragrant torches and incense will live in the soul's memory, the light will live on in remembrance, a glimmer of heavenly light?

10

Is it a dream? Is the daylight a dream, the daylight that floods him when the people move away from the entrance to the cave, when a door opened in the wall of the crowd standing around and a new light appeared, without doubt divine, a forgotten light, at once remote and close, the light of a sunlit day, the light of life and clear sight?

At first there was nothing but the blue vault of the sky, far off, luminous in its own glow, sky-blue, far above his head, a sky-blue sea, calm and serene, swelled by high tide; then in the mild blue of the sky he thinks he can see a few white clouds, not heavenly sheep, not a flock, a white, heavenly flock out to graze, but wisps of white wool floating with the tide of the blue vault, just enough to keep the human eye, his eye, from doubting the blue of the sky, just enough to keep his soul from wandering.

For this was without doubt the light of God's day and it was without doubt the blue light of the sky or the light of his ascension to heaven. Or was this too a dream, the flash that shut his eyes before he was quite out of the cave, rocking on the carriers' powerful shoulders as in a boat, the light spattering him like water, his soul sinking into the glittering blue wave as into holy water, neck deep, the light engulfing him in a warm bliss that emanated from a distant memory of his soul, a distant vision, the light lashing at his eyes like an illumination and like the flame of angels' wings, while he presses his eyes shut, presses until they ache, not from the darkness now or the visions but from the light? And he feels the difference, feels it behind his tightly shut eyes, for in his consciousness, somewhere in the middle of his forehead, somewhere behind the frontal bone, in the center, there between his eyes, at the base of the optic nerve and at the heart of vision itself, purple disks began to quiver, purple and crimson, and blue and yellow and green, then red again, and it was without doubt light and not an illusion, or perhaps only an optical illusion, but it was light!

11

Unless that too, alas, was a dream, a bodily illusion, an optical illusion, the illusion of a sleepwalker who has overstepped the bounds and borders of night and moon, of daybreak and moonlight, and stepped into day and the light of the rising sun, the eternal divinity in eternal conflict with the goddess Luna, and now – lo! – coming to disperse the illusory, the specious light of the deposed goddess, its much hated foe; but it was light! Not the flickering, feeble light that gnaws and chafes itself, ignites and snuffs itself, pursues and smothers itself, consuming itself in its own flame and smoke, its own quiver and flight, its own coals and embers; yes, truly it was light!

Not cold moonlight but broad daylight, the light of the sun piercing his tightly shut lids, a crimson flame infiltrating the thick mat of his lashes, the pores of his skin, the light of day felt on each part of the body that emerged from the cold darkness of the cave, a warm light and salutary, the life-giving light of God's day!

Unless that too, alas, was a dream?

The crimson rushing into his blood, his heart pounding, and the blood coursing through his body, warm and jubilant, blood suddenly crimson and vigorous; the warm mantle of sun he wrapped around himself as if it were his own warm skin, a light gold mantle of sun covering his body, his icy wet hairshirt overlain with sumptuous silk.

Or was this, too, a dream, the new earthly scent penetrating his nostrils long dulled by sleep and repose, the warm scent of the earth, the scent of grass, of vegetation, the blessed breath of light and life which after the musty air of the cave was as sweet as an apple?

Could that too have been a dream? The blessed libation of

his spirit and his body, the blaze that kept him from opening his eyes, for it smote him on the forehead with such force that the light turned to darkness, red and yellow, blue and crimson and green darkness, and he had to keep his eyes tight shut, for the warm red darkness behind his eyelids made him feel as if he had plunged his head into boiling sacrificial blood.

12

Like a child in its cradle or on its mother's back, he rocked on the shoulders of his carriers – a child asleep on its mother's back, in a field, the sun beating down, eyes closed in blissful languor, feeling only the warmth of the sunlight on its skin, on its heavy limbs, through its tightly shut lids.

Stunned by the great light and the smells, on the border between consciousness and unconsciousness, he listened to the prayers and chants of the pilgrims, the angelic chorus of children's voices, and the squeal of instruments, the whine of the citharas, the pipes' lament, and let the resounding anthems and angels' trumpet blasts flow over him.

Washed with ever-multiplying voices, voices of the crowd, lamentations and sobs, curses and entreaties, borne on the wings of ever-multiplying smells, smells of the crowd and of sweat penetrating his nostrils at the moment when warm red blood of the sun starts streaming through the iceberg of his body embalmed by clammy darkness, he suddenly catches the odor of his carriers, the odor of their shaven heads and pungent armpits, and then the forgotten odor of cattle as they were lifted, all three of them, onto an ox-drawn cart spread with a soft sheepskin.

His head propped on soft pillows, he lay in the cart as in a boat and listened to the creak of the wheels, slow and lazy, mingled with chanting and wailing. Once, half opening his tightly shut lids, letting in the daylight, which made a painful incision in the eyeball, like a steel blade, he looked about him, to left and right, and saw the faces of his friend Malchus and of John, mute, expressionless faces, like his own face undoubtedly, saw them staring, like him, with half-open eyes at the blue of the firmament, the wonder of creation.

Was that, too, a dream? The warm motionlessness and sudden calm, the child-like, animal-like submission to sun and daylight, and the eyes turned toward the vault of heaven, heaven's blue vault, now cloudless, the oblivion-blue, regeneration-blue, miracle-blue vault of heaven. Was that, too, a dream?

And he felt the joy of his body after the dank, slimy, viscid shell of darkness has fallen away, the childlike joy of the flesh, of entrails and bones, a joy of bone marrow and brain marrow, a bestial amphibian joy, a reptilian joy, when the body in labour delivers itself from the slough of darkness, the shell of dankness and moisture, the brittle skin of damp and timeless blackness that seeps through pores, damp and timeless, to the sensitive, bloody layer beneath the skin and, like a serpent's venom, permeates the body, its flesh and bones and bone marrow, following the same paths as the cart and the warm light of the sun.

Was this too a dream? The sunbath wringing darkness from the marrow of his bones, the fumes rising from his body as it oozed the serpent's green venom through its pores, making room for the light of life, the life-giving sap that would make his blood red again.

Was that, too, a dream, the moment when the heavy rocks of his cave-tomb opened before him and he was dazzled by heavenly light?

13

Back in the darkness of the cave, he could recollect it all with painful clarity, for his icy body remembered the warmth, his blood remembered the light, his eye remembered the blue of the heavens, his ear recalled the singing and the pipes.

And now, behold! All was silence again, all was eclipse again, all was torpor and numbness, absence of movement and absence of light, yet he remembers *the light*, remembers it with a shudder of carnal yearning, the very memory of it makes him quiver, as when the sunlight touched him in that dream or that reality, the sun perched on his shoulders, embraced his loins, when in that dream or that reality the sun sowed its seed in his viscera, rippled through his blood, warmed his bones.

And now – behold! – all is once again nothing but a tomb of the body and a dungeon of the soul, a realm of darkness, a palace of mold, green mold, infusing his heart and skin, bone marrow and brain marrow, and in vain he reaches out to touch the moist and icy stone of the cave with his dry, swollen fingers, in vain does he lift his eyelids, in vain touch them with his fingers to test whether it was not all a dream, an illusion, the silence dotted with the dripping of invisible drops from the invisible vaults of the cave, the darkness riddled by a muted murmur, in vain does he strain to hear the singing and the whine of the pipes, the singing that he remembered so vividly, that his body remembers.

Nothing. Nothing but the empty echo of memory and the resonant silence of the cave; the sound of silence, the stillness of time. The light of darkness. The water of dream. Water.

14

Jolting along, the cart entered the town, and high above his head rose the vaults of the town gates, cleaving the blue of the heavens with their white stone arches, bridges spanning invisible banks, stone arches within reach of the hands lying motionless at the sides of his numb, all but lifeless body.

Here and there, where the stone had cracked, a blade of grass sprouted from the arches, two or three blades of green grass, or some roots, white and split down the middle, or the rust-colored frond of a wild fern emerging from the heart of the stone. No, it was no dream! The sun streaked with shadows beneath the arches of the town gates, the fern, the grass, the moss within each of his hands – no, surely it was not a dream.

For one can dream water, fire, and sky; one can dream man and woman, especially woman; one can dream dreams in reality and dreams in a dream; but surely this was not a dream, this white chiseled stone, these vaults, this fortress town.

15

Creaking and jolting, the ox-drawn cart took them under the arches of the town gates and through the shadows of the houses lining the streets, yet he barely saw the houses, for he stared straight up, his eyes glassy and motionless with wonder or sleep, merely sensing the stone presence of the stone houses, the lofty houses, on either side of him, left and right, whenever a shadow fell on his face and tired eyes, but he also sensed the stone presence of the tumbledown huts, which did not block the sun but were no less present, invisible but solid and real, more real than the sky above his head, more real than the creak of the yoke and the voices of the crowd still accompanying them, murmuring prayers and singing psalms.

16

'O thou who art blessed, thou shalt stand before the Emperor!' No, it was no dream. He could still recall the voice, perhaps not the face, but the voice bursting with exaltation, a voice cracking with fear or fervor. 'O thou who art blessed!'

And lying there motionless, in the cart, he saw the red beard and light blue eyes of a young man leaning over him, from behind, in such a way that his face, upside down, hovered directly above him and blocked the sun. 'O thou who art blessed!' Was the young man saying that to him, Dionysius, or were dream and reality still toying with his consciousness?

Staring into the young man's eyes, he noted with mistrust

that they were observing and following his own, timidly and apprehensively perhaps, but with a certain youthful insolence.

And looking up at him mutely, Dionysius saw his thin lips and red beard begin to move, and he read the words from those lips before his ears brought them to his consciousness: 'O thou who art blessed!'

Was it not mockery and scorn? Was it not the voice of his dream, the voice of his illusions?

And Dionysius said, 'Who art thou?' – his voice emerging abruptly, scarcely audible. The insolence in those light blue eyes now seemed to have vanished, and the young man quickly turned away, his red-tipped eyelashes coming down over his eyes and his lips beginning to move again.

'O thou who art blessed! I am thy slave and the slave of thy master!'

Were they, too, a dream? Those stuttering lips, that quivering beard?

'Decius is not my master!' he uttered, expecting a lion's roar in return. But lo! just as he closed his eyes the better to hear the lion roar, the face of the young man with the red beard vanished, leaving only the vast heavens spread out above him.

17

All at once there was silence, broken only by the monotonous singing and keening of the people: the creak of the wheels jolting along the bumpy, winding road had ceased; the cart had come to a halt.

Was that, too, a dream? The calm suddenly descending upon his soul after a long muddle of voices and strange happenings – was that, too, a dream? The voices of the crowd had died down to nothing, and the creak of the cart had ceased, and the whine and scrape of the wheels. The sun's rays, which until then had fallen at an angle on his face, were gone, screened by an awning he could not see. His body rested on a soft sheepskin, and the odor of wool seeped into his nostrils, and the odor of cypress and the odor of the sun-drenched day and the warm, intoxicating odors of the sea.

Lulled until then, like an infant in its cradle, by the whine of the wheels and the sway of the cart, his numb body, his light bones, his empty innards, his quiet heart, his dry skin all surrendered to the serenity of easy breathing; he felt like a child who had just been awakened.

No, it was no dream – that serenity, that radiance!

18

Even before looking to left and right, even before wondering whether it was all a dream, even before apprehending the miraculous ascension of his body in this scented bath of a summer's day, he remembered sweet Prisca's name and at once his body was flooded with bliss and the air with the scent of roses.

Oh, joy!

And the mere recollection of his body and heart during that moment of serenity, that wave of exaltation, there, before the palace gate, when the voices of the crowd had died down and the creak of the cart had ceased, when Prisca's sweet name is engraved on his soul and exudes a rose-like aroma – now, once more, in the darkness of the cave, the tomb of eternity, it awakens in him a vague and distant elation, grazing him with its breath, and his body is flooded with light and heat from afar; but then all returns to anguish of the spirit and the darkness of time.

19

He lay in the darkness of the cave, vainly straining his eyes, vainly calling to his friend Malchus, vainly calling to John, the saintly shepherd, vainly calling to the green-eyed dog Qitmir, vainly calling to the Lord his God: the darkness was as thick as tar, the silence – the silence of the tomb of eternity. All he could hear was the dripping of water from invisible vaults, the grinding of eternity in the clepsydra of time.

Oh, who can divide dream from reality, day from night, night from dawn, memory from illusion?

Who can draw a sharp line between sleep and death?

Who, O Lord, can draw a sharp dividing line between present, past, and future?

Who, O Lord, can separate the joy of love from the sadness of memory?

Happy are they who hope, O Lord, for their hopes shall be fulfilled.

Happy are they who know what is day and what is night, O Lord, for they shall revel in the day and revel in the night and the repose thereof.

Happy are they for whom the past has been, the present is, and the future will be, O Lord, for their lives shall flow like water.

Happy are they who dream by night and recall their dreams by day, O Lord, for they shall rejoice.

Happy are they who know by day where they have been by night, O Lord, for theirs is the day and theirs is the night.

Happy are they who recall not their nocturnal wanderings, O Lord, for theirs shall be the light of day.

20

They lay on their backs in a dark cave on Mount Celius, with their hands crossed in prayer like corpses, all three of them, Dionysius and his friend Malchus and, a short distance away, John, the saintly shepherd, and his dog, Qitmir.

They slept the lifeless sleep of the dead.

Had you come upon them in that condition, you would surely have turned and fled; fear would have turned you to stone.

Simon Magus

Seventeen years after the death and miraculous resurrection of Jesus the Nazarene, a man named Simon appeared on the dusty roads that crisscross Samaria and vanish in the desert beneath the fickle sands, a man whom his disciples called the Magus and his enemies derided as 'the Borborite'. Some claimed he had come from a miserable Samarian village named Gitta, others that he was from Syria or Anatolia. It cannot be denied that he himself contributed to the confusion, answering the most innocent questions about his origins with a wave of the hand broad enough to take in both the neighboring hamlet and half the horizon.

He was brawny and of medium height, and his black curly hair had begun to thin at the top; his beard, also curly and unkempt, was flecked with gray. He had a hooked, bony nose and a sheep-like profile. One of his eyes was larger than the other, giving his face a somewhat sarcastic expression. In his left ear he wore a gold earring: a snake swallowing its tail. His waist was wound several times around with a flaxen rope, which served as a prop for his circus tricks: suddenly it would rise straight into the air, and he would scramble up it – before the spectators' wondering eyes – as he might scramble up a bean pole. Or he would tie it around the neck of a calf and then, uttering a magic formula, chop its head off with a single slice of the sword. For a moment, head and body lay severed in the desert sand, but then the miracle worker pronounced the magic formula – backwards, this time – and the head reattached itself to the body. Picking up the rope, which had remained in the sand, he would undo the knot and wind it around his waist again, unless a member of the audience wished to verify the fiber's composition. He would then hand him one end of the stiff rope as if offering him a stick; the moment the skeptic took hold of it, it would go limp and fall to the earth, raising a cloud of dust.

He was as fluent in Greek and Coptic as he was in Aramaic and Hebrew, and knew various local dialects, though his enemies claimed he spoke each of the languages with a strong accent. Simon paid scant heed to such rumors and even gave the impression of encouraging them. He was said to be quickwitted and an excellent orator, especially when addressing disciples and followers or the crowds that flocked to hear him. 'Then his eyes would shine like stars,' said one of his disciples. 'He had the voice of a lunatic and the eye of a lecher,' one of his adversaries remarked.

Along the tangled roads leading from East to West and West to East, Simon Magus crossed paths with a great many preachers. The disciples of John and Paul – and John and Paul themselves – were then engaged in spreading the word of Jesus the Nazarene, whose memory was still alive in Palestine, Judaea, and Samaria; and Simon frequently discovered their sandal tracks at the entrance to a village. The village would be strangely peaceful at that time of day, the only noise the barking of a dog or the resonant bleating of a sheep. Then, itself very much like braying, came the distant sound of male voices, resonant and clear, though as yet not quite intelligible. They belonged to the Apostles, who, perched on wobbly barrels, were preaching the perfection of the world and of God's Creation. Simon would hide in the shade of a hovel, waiting for them to depart, and enter the village before the people had completely dispersed.

Then, surrounded by his escort, he would himself begin to preach. Worn out by the subtle reasoning of the Apostles, the crowd was less than eager to gather round. 'We've just seen off Paul and John,' they would say to him. 'We've had enough words for a year.'

'I am not an Apostle,' Simon would say. 'I am one of you. They place their hands on your heads to inspire you with the Holy Ghost; I hold out my hands to raise you up from the dust.' Whereupon he would lift his arms skywards, his wide sleeves sliding down in graceful folds to reveal a pair of beautiful white hands and the fine fingers found only among idlers and illusionists.

'They offer you eternal salvation,' Simon would go on. 'I offer you knowledge and the desert. Anyone who wants can join me.'

The people were used to every kind of wanderer from

every direction, though mostly from the East – now alone, now in pairs, now accompanied by a crowd of believers. Some left their mules and camels outside the village or at the foot of the mountain or in the next valley; others arrived with an armed escort (and their sermons were more like threats or playacting); still others rode in on their mules and, without even dismounting, launched into acrobatic tricks. But for the past fifteen years or so, since the death of a certain Nazarene, the visitors had tended to be young and healthy, with carefully trimmed beards or no beards at all, and wore white cloaks, carried shepherd's staffs, and called themselves Apostles and sons of God. Their sandals were dusty from the long journey, their words so much alike they seemed to have been learned from the same book; they all referred to the same miracle, which they had themselves witnessed: the Nazarene had turned water into wine before their eyes and fed a large crowd with a few sardines. Some claimed to have seen Him rise up to the sky in a dazzling light and reach heaven like a dove. The blind, whom they brought with them as living witnesses, claimed that the light had taken away their sight but given them spiritual enlightenment.

And they all called themselves sons of God and sons of the Son of God. For a chunk of bread and a jug of wine they promised bliss and life everlasting; and when the people chased them from their doors, setting their fierce dogs upon them, the preachers threatened them with everlasting hell where their flesh would burn over a low flame like a lamb on the spit.

There were, however, fine speakers among them, men who knew how to give the suspicious crowds and the even more suspicious authorities answers to numerous complex questions concerning not only the soul but the body, animal husbandry and farming. They cured young men of pimples and advised young girls in the hygiene of preserving their virginity and bearing it more easily; they counseled the elderly about preparation for death, about what words to utter at their mortal hour and how to cross their arms to slip through the narrows leading to the light; they told mothers how to save their progeny without expensive sorcerers and potions, and how to keep their sons from going to war; they taught barren women clear and simple prayers to say three times a day on an empty stomach so that the Holy Ghost – as they called it – might make their wombs fruitful.

And they did it all for nothing, at no cost, excepting the crust of bread they gratefully accepted or the bowl of cool water they drank in small gulps, murmuring incomprehensible words. From the four corners of the earth they came, one after the other, with various customs and tongues, with beards and without, but all bearing more or less the same message, one confirming what the other proclaimed, and apart from a slight variation in detail and a few minor inconsistencies, the tale of the miracles and resurrection of the Nazarene began to gain authenticity. The people of Judaea, Samaria, and Anatolia grew accustomed to the peaceable young men in dusty sandals who crossed their hands over their chests, spoke in virginal voices, and sang with their eyes raised to heaven.

They gave the young men cool water and crusts of bread, and the young men thanked them and promised them life everlasting, describing a miraculous place they would gain after death, a land where there was no desert, no sand, no snakes or spiders, only broad-fronded palms, springs with ice-cold water, grass that grew to knee-level, and above, a mild sun, nights like days and days that never ended; a land where cows grazed, goats and sheep browsed in the pastures, flowers smelled sweet all year round, spring lasted forever, where there were no crows, no eagles, only nightingales that sang all day. And so on.

This picture of the gardens of paradise, which everyone initially regarded as ridiculous and impossible (who had ever seen a place where the sun always shone and there was no pain or death?) – this picture the gentle, blue-eyed young men evoked with such conviction, such inspiration, that people came to believe them. When a lie is repeated long enough, people start believing it. Because people need faith. Many young men donned long-laced sandals and set off with them. Some returned to their villages after a year or two, others after ten years. They returned exhausted from their long journeys, their beards speckled with white. They spoke softly now too, their hands crossed over their loins. They spoke of His miracles, of His teaching, they preached His strange laws, scorned the pleasures of the flesh, dressed modestly, ate moderately, and used both hands to raise the chalice to their lips when drinking wine. Yet if someone contradicted them, if someone cast doubt on their teaching and His miracles, if someone – woe unto him! – questioned the life everlasting and the gardens of paradise, then they would fly into a sudden rage. They would describe the tortures of eternal expiation with vigorous and violent words, menacing and fiery words. 'May the gods keep you,' a pagan wrote, 'from their evil tongues and imprecations.'

They knew how to win over skeptics with flattery and promises, bribes and threats; and the more their power spread and their followers increased, the stronger and more arrogant they grew. They blackmailed families, sowed discord in the minds of individuals, hatched plots against anyone who expressed the slightest mistrust of their doctrine. They had their own fire-brands and rabble-rousers, their own secret tribunals at which they pronounced maledictions and sentences, burned the writings of their enemies, and cast anathemas on the heads of recalcitrants. People joined them in ever-increasing numbers because they rewarded the faithful and punished the rebellious.

It was at this time that Simon, called the Magus, made his appearance.

Simon preached that the God of the Apostles was a tyrant and that a tyrant could not be God to thinking men. Their God – Jehovah, Elohim – abominates mankind, chokes it, slaughters it, visits pestilences and wild beasts upon it, serpents and tarantulas, lions and tigers, thunder and lightning, plagues, leprosy, syphilis, tempests and gales, droughts and floods, nightmares and sleeplessness, the sorrows of youth and the impotence of age. He has allotted our blessed ancestors a place in the gardens of paradise, but deprived them of the sweetest fruit, the only one that man deserves, the only one that distinguishes him from the dog, the camel, the ass, and the monkey – the knowledge of good and evil.

'And when our unfortunate ancestor, driven by curiosity, wished to seize that fruit, what did their Elohim, your Elohim, the Just, the Great, the All-Powerful – what did he do then? Eh?' Simon shouted, teetering on the wobbly barrel. 'You know very well. (Your apostles – his servants and slaves – tell you in their sermons day after day.) He chased him off like a leper, a pariah, chased him mercilessly, with a fiery sword. And why? Because he is a God of animosity, of hatred and jealousy. In place of freedom he preaches slavery, in place of pleasure deprivation, in place of knowledge dogma . . . O people of Samaria, has not your vindictive God destroyed your houses? Has he not inflicted drought and locusts upon your fields? Has he not turned out dozens of your leprous neighbors? Did he not, only a year ago, lay waste to your village with a terrible plague? What kind of God is he, what kind of justice is his – for your apostles call him just – if he continues even now to wreak his vengeance on you for a so-called sin committed by distant ancestors? What kind of justice is his if he visits plagues, thunder and lightning, pestilence, sorrow, and misfortune upon you for no other reason than that your ancestors, driven by curiosity, by that living fire which engenders knowledge, dared to pluck the apple? No, people of Samaria, he is no God; he is an avenger, he is a brigand, an outlaw, who with his angelic hosts – armed to the teeth, armed with fiery swords and poisoned arrows – stands in your path. When your figs ripen, he sends down a blight upon them; and when your olives ripen, he sends down a storm to tear them from the trees and hail to pound them into the dirt and turn them to mud; when your sheep bring forth a lamb, he visits a plague upon them or wolves or tigers to devastate the fold; and when you have a child, he visits convulsions upon it to cut short its life. What kind of God is he, what kind of justice is his if he does all this? No, that is not God, that is not the One who is in heaven, that is not Elohim; that is someone else. For Elohim the Creator of heaven and earth, of man and woman, of every fowl of the air and everything that creepeth upon the earth, the Creator of every living thing, the One who raised up the mountains above the seas, the One who created the seas and the rivers and the oceans, the green grasses and the shade of the palm tree, sun and rain, air and fire – *that* is Elohim, the God of justice. And the one whose teachings Peter and John and Paul and their disciples have taught you – he is a brigand and a murderer. And all that John and Paul, James and Peter tell you about him and his kingdom – hear, O people of Samaria! – is a lie. Their chosen land is a lie, their God a lie, their miracles false. They lie, because their God, to whom they swear allegiance, is false; they lie incessantly and, having thus entered into a great maelstrom of lies, no longer even realize they are lying. Where everyone lies, no one lies; where everything is lies, nothing is a lie. The kingdom of heaven, the kingdom of justice is a lie. Every attribute of their God is a lie. That he is righteous – a lie. Truth-loving – a lie. One and

Only – a lie. Immortal – a lie. Their scriptures are false because they promise lies; they promise paradise, and paradise is a lie because it is in their hands, because they are the ones who stand at the gates of paradise, their angels with fiery swords and their judges with false scales.'

The people listened to him with indifference and mistrust, as a crowd listens to demagogues – seeking hidden meanings behind obscure words. For they were accustomed to hearing the authorities, the Pharisees, men with power, use sweet-sounding promises to conceal wiles, threats, and extortions, and expected this man, too, to declare his intentions, to state at last why he had come, to give the reason for his empty words, his vague and confusing prattle. That is why they kept listening. And because they hoped he would cap his muddled remarks with an acrobatic trick or a miracle.

'The kingdom of heaven rests on a foundation of lies,' Simon continued, staring into the merciless sun, 'and its roof has two slopes: white lies and black lies. Their scriptures are composed of false words and mysterious laws, and each law is a lie: ten laws, ten lies . . . It is not enough that their Elohim is a tyrant, a vindictive tyrant, and as cross as a crotchety old man; no, they want everyone to venerate him, to fall at his feet, to think of nothing else but him! To call him, that tyrant, the One and Only, All-Powerful, and Righteous God. And to submit to him alone! Who are they, O people of Samaria, these charlatans who come to you and fill your ears with lies and false promises? They are people who have secured his mercy for themselves and wish you to submit without a murmur, to suffer all the trials of existence – torments, pestilences, quakes, floods, plagues – without cursing him. Why else would he forbid you to take his name in vain? They are lies, all lies, I tell you! The things you hear from Peter and Paul, the white lies and the black lies of his disciples – they are all one big, dreadful hoax! Whence: thou shalt not kill! Killing is what he does, their One and Only, All-Powerful, and Righteous God! He is the one who smites infants in their cradles and mothers in childbirth and toothless old men! Killing is his vocation. Whence: thou shalt not kill! Leave the killing to him and his! They are the only ones called to it! They are destined to be wolves, you to be sheep! You must give yourselves up to their laws! . . . Whence: thou shalt not commit adultery, that they may carry off the flower of thy womanhood. And whence: thou shalt not covet thy neighbor's goods, for thou hast no reason to envy him. They demand everything of you – soul and body, spirit and thought – and give you promises in exchange; for your current submission and your current prayers and your current silence they give you a crazy quilt of false promises: they promise you the future, a future that does not exist . . .'

Simon did not notice, or merely pretended not to notice, that the people had dispersed and that his only remaining audience consisted of those who called themselves his disciples. All the while, his faithful companion Sophia had been wiping the sweat from his forehead and passing him a pitcher of water, which had turned lukewarm even though she had kept it deep in the sand.

Sophia was a small woman of about thirty, with thick hair and dark eyes like sloes. Over her bright, translucent cloak she wore colorful silk scarves, probably purchased in India. Simon's disciples described her as the epitome of wisdom and mature womanly beauty, while the Christian pilgrims spread all sorts of rumors about her; namely, that she was a flirt, a tramp, a tease, a hussy, and an impostor who had found grace in the eyes of her impostor of a companion in a Syrian brothel. Simon never denied it. Her former life as a slave and concubine served him as an obvious example, example and lesson, of Jehovah's brutality and the cruelty of this world. That Fallen Angel, that Stray Sheep, he maintained, was merely a victim of God's brutality, a Pure Soul imprisoned in human flesh, her spirit having migrated for centuries from vessel to vessel, from body to body, from shadow to shadow. She was Lot's daughter and she was Rachel and she was Fair Helen. (In other words, the Greeks and the barbarians had admired a shadow and shed blood over a phantom!) Her most recent incarnation had been as a prostitute in the Syrian bawdy house.

'But meanwhile,' Simon continued, after spitting out a mouthful of the lukewarm water when he glimpsed a band of pilgrims in white cloaks emerging from the shade of the houses, men in whom he recognized Peter and his disciples armed with shepherd's staffs. 'But meanwhile – beneath the murky shroud of the heavens, within the dark walls of the earth, and in the dungeon of existence – despise wealth, as they teach you, deny the pleasures of the flesh, and scorn woman, that cup of nectar, that urn of bliss, in the name of their false paradise and out of fear of their false hell, as if this life were not hell . . .'

'Some choose the earthly kingdom, others the kingdom of heaven,' said Peter, leaning on his staff with both hands.

'Only he who has known wealth may despise it,' said Simon, squinting his larger eye at Peter. 'Only he who has known poverty may admire it. Only he who has experienced the pleasures of the flesh may deny them.'

'The Son of God experienced suffering,' said Peter.

'His miracles are proof of His righteousness,' one of Peter's disciples interjected.

'Miracles are no proof of righteousness,' Simon responded. 'Miracles serve as proof only for the gullible, the multitude. They are nothing but a craze introduced by your miserable Jew, the one who ended on the cross.'

'Only he who has the power to perform miracles may speak as you do,' Peter objected.

Then Simon jumped down from the wobbly barrel and landed eye-to-eye with his challenger. 'I will now fly up to the sky,' he said.

'I should like to see it,' Peter replied, with a quiver in his voice.

'I know the extent of my power,' said Simon, 'and I know I cannot reach the seventh heaven. But I shall go through six. Only thought can reach the seventh, because the seventh heaven is all light and bliss. And bliss is denied mortal man.'

'Enough philosophizing,' said one of Peter's disciples. 'If you reach even that cloud up there, we shall respect you as we do the Nazarene.'

Hearing that there were some unusual doings afoot just outside the village, near the large olive tree, and that the chatterbox was at last about to do one of his fakir's tricks, a crowd gathered round again.

'Don't be gone too long,' one of the spectators called out mockingly. 'In fact, why not leave something behind as security?'

Simon unwound the flaxen rope from his waist and placed it at his feet. 'It is all I have.'

And Sophia said, 'Take this scarf. It's cold up there, as cold as at the bottom of a well.' And she put the scarf around his neck.

'These preparations are taking too long,' said Peter.

'He is waiting for the sun to go down,' added one of Peter's disciples, 'so he can run for it under cover of night.'

'Goodbye,' said Simon, kissing Sophia on the forehead.

'Farewell,' said one of Peter's disciples. 'Watch out you don't catch cold!'

Suddenly Simon jumped with both legs, like a cockerel, flapping his arms clumsily, and dust spread around his sandals.

'Cock-a-doodle-doo!' a joker cried, a smooth-cheeked young man with shrewd eyes that turned to slanting slits when he laughed.

Simon glanced over in his direction and said, 'It's not so easy, my boy! The earth exerts a hold on all bodies, on the merest feather, to say nothing of a human wreck of more than a hundredweight.'

Peter was unable to stifle his laughter at Simon's sophistry, and had to hide it in his beard.

'If you were as good at flying as you are at philosophy,' said the joker, 'you'd be soaring through the clouds by now.'

'Philosophizing is easier than flying, I admit,' said Simon, with sorrow in his voice. 'Even you know how to chatter, though never once in your miserable life have you wrenched yourself so much as a foot off the ground . . . And now let me collect my strength and my thoughts and concentrate with everything I have on the horror of our earthly existence, on the imperfection of the world, on the myriad lives torn asunder, on the beasts that devour one another, on the snake that bites a stag as it grazes in the shade, on the wolves that slaughter sheep, on the mantises that consume their males, on the bees that die after they sting, on the mothers who labor to bring us into the world, on the blind kittens children toss into rivers, on the terror of the fish in the whale's entrails and the terror of the beaching whale, on the sadness of an elephant dying of old age, on the butterfly's fleeting joy, on the deceptive beauty of the flower, on the fleeting illusion of a lovers' embrace, on the horror of spilt seed, on the impotence of the aging tiger, on the rotting of teeth in the mouth, on the myriad dead leaves lining the forest floor, on the fear of the fledgling when its mother pushes it out of the nest, on the infernal torture of the worm baking in the sun as if roasting in living fire, on the anguish of a lovers' parting, on the horror known by lepers, on the hideous metamorphoses of women's breasts, on wounds, on the pain of the blind . . .'

And all at once they saw the mortal body of Simon Magus detach itself from the ground, rise straight up, higher and higher, arms beating like fish gills, subtly, almost imperceptibly, hair and beard streaming in gentle flight, floating.

Not a cry, not a breath could be heard in the silence that suddenly settled upon the crowd. They stood stock-still, as if dumbfounded, their gaze fixed on the sky. Even the blind rolled their vacant, milky eyes upwards, for they, too, had grasped what the sudden silence meant, where the crowd had directed its attention, where all heads were turned.

Peter stood petrified too, his mouth open in amazement. He did not believe in miracles other than miracles of faith, and miracles could come from Him alone, the sole Miracle Worker, the One who had turned water into wine; all others were merely magic tricks, a matter of concealed ropes. Miracles were granted only to Christians, and among Christians only to those whose faith was as solid as a rock, like His.

Shaken for a moment, frightened by the illusion – for it could be nothing more than a sensory illusion, a case of Egyptian fairground sorcery – he rubbed his eyes, then looked over at the spot where Simon, called the Magus, had been standing (and therefore ought still to be standing). But he was not there, only his flaxen rope all coiled up like a snake, and the dust, now slowly settling, that Simon had stirred up as he hopped up and down like a clumsy rooster, flapping his arms like clipped wings. Then he raised his eyes to where the crowd's heads pointed, and again he saw the Magus. His silhouette stood out clearly against the white cloud. It looked like a gigantic eagle, but it was not an eagle; it was a man: the human arms, human legs, human head were still easily discernible, though, to tell the truth, whether the man approaching the cloud was actually Simon Magus was impossible to ascertain, because the facial features were beyond recognition.

Peter looked up at the white cloud and blinked to banish the illusion that had duped the entire crowd. For if the black silhouette approaching the cloud was in fact Simon, then His miracles and the truth of the Christian faith were *but one of the truths of this world* and not the sole truth, then the world was a mystery and faith an illusion, then his life had lost its foundation, then man was a mystery among mysteries, then the unity of the world and Creation was an unknown.

What must be – if he could believe his eyes – the mortal body of Simon Magus had now reached the cloud, a black speck that vanished for a moment, then stood out clearly against the low cloud's base, and finally disappeared for good in the white mist.

The silence lasted only a moment before it was broken by a sigh of wonder in the crowd; people fell on their knees, prostrated themselves, and rolled their heads as if in a trance. Even some of Peter's disciples bowed before the new pagan miracle they had just witnessed.

Then Peter closed his eyes and said, in Hebrew (because it is the natural language of saints, and lest the crowd should understand him), the following prayer: 'Our One and Only Father, who art in heaven, come to the aid of my senses, which have been deceived by a mirage; grant unto mine eyes keenness of sight and unto my mind the wisdom to avoid dreams and illusions and remain steadfast in Thy faith and in my love for Thy Son, Our Saviour. Amen.'

And God said unto him, 'Follow my counsel, O faithful servant. Say unto the people that the power of faith is greater than the snares of the senses; say it loudly, so that all may hear. And say unto them, loud, so that all may hear: God is one and His name is Elohim, and the Son of God is one and His name is Jesus, and faith is one and it is the Christian faith. And he who has just now soared up to the sky, Simon, called the Magus, is an apostate and a desecrator of God's teachings; he has indeed taken flight by dint of his will and his thoughts and is now flying, invisible, to the stars, borne by doubt and human curiosity, which, however, have their limits. And say unto them, loud, so that all may hear, that I was the One who granted him the power of temptation, that all his might and strength came from me, for it was I who suffered him to tempt Christian souls with his miracles, that I might show them there is no miracle without me, no power but mine. Speak thus unto them and have no fear.'

Then Peter opened his eyes, climbed up a mound of dried manure swarming with flies, and began to shout at the top of his voice, 'Listen, people, and hear!'

No one paid any attention to him. The people lay with their heads in the dust, as sheep lie in the shade of a grove on a hot day.

Again Peter shouted at the top of his voice, 'Listen, O people of Samaria, listen to what I have to tell you.'

A few people lifted their heads, the blind first.

'You have seen what you have seen. You have been the victims of a sensory illusion. That conjurer, that fakir who received his training in Egypt . . .'

'He kept his word,' said Sophia.

'By the time I count to ten,' Peter went on, taking no notice of her, 'his body will crash to the earth he so despised, fall like a stone at your feet, never again to rise from the dust . . . For God the One and Only so desires. One . . .'

'He flew, didn't he?' said Sophia. 'He proved he was a magus.'

'Two . . .'

'Even if he falls, he is the victor,' said Sophia.

Peter kept his eyes shut while he counted, as if wishing to gain time.

And then he heard a shriek going up from the crowd, and he opened his eyes. At the very spot where Simon had disappeared, a black speck was emerging from the cloud and starting to grow. The body of Simon Magus came hurtling to the earth like a stone, spinning on its longitudinal and transversal axes. As it grew bigger and more visible, the arms and legs could be seen flailing, and the crowd started running in all directions, apparently out of fear that the body plunging headlong from the heavens would land on one of their number.

From then on, everything happened very quickly. Like a sack of moist sand when it lands on the drayman's cart or like a sheep dropped by an eagle in flight, the body of Simon Magus crashed to the ground.

The first to approach it was Sophia the prostitute, his faithful companion. All she wanted was to cover his eyes with the scarf she had given him, but forced to close her own eyes at the horrible spectacle, she was unable to do even that. He lay on the ground, his skull fractured, his limbs broken, his face mutilated and streaming with blood, his intestines protruding like the entrails of a slaughtered ox; on the ground lay a heap of crushed, shattered bones and mangled flesh, and his burnoose, his sandals, and her scarf were entangled with the flesh and bones in a revolting mangled mess.

The people who came up to look at the sight heard Sophia say in tones of malediction, 'This is yet further proof of the truth of *his* teaching. Man's life is a Fall, and a hell, and the world is in the hands of tyrants. Cursed be the greatest of all tyrants, Elohim.'

Then she made for the desert, wailing.

2

According to another version, Simon Magus did not direct his challenge at the seventh heaven, but at the earth, the greatest of all Illusions.

So Simon lay on his back, his hands behind his head, in the shade of a giant olive tree, staring up at the sky, at 'the horror of the heavens.' The prostitute sat at his side, 'with her legs spread wide like a pregnant cow,' as a Christian polemist notes (though we cannot be certain whether he is reporting his own observations or citing an eyewitness – or simply making it all up). The olive tree and its meager shade remain the only hard facts amid the multifarious evidence in the curious story of Simon's miracles. And so, chance willed it that Peter and his men should come upon him there. Doubtless provoked by Sophia's unworthy bearing, one of the disciples, his head turned away to shield him from temptation, asked Simon whether it was better to sow on earth and reap in heaven or to cast one's seed to the wind – a scholastic question requiring an unambiguous answer.

Simon propped himself up on one elbow and, rising no farther, answered him over his shoulder, saying: *'All earth is earth, and where one sows is all the same. True communion comes from the commingling of man and woman.'*

'Any man and any woman?' Peter asked, nearly turning around in amazement.

'Woman is the urn of bliss,' said Simon. 'And you, like all dimwits, you stop up your ears to keep them free of blasphemy; you avert your gaze or flee when you have no answer.'

There followed a long theological discussion of Elohim, punishment, repentance, abnegation, soul and body, and the meaning of life, all of which was interspersed with scholastic arguments and quotations in Hebrew, Greek, Coptic, and Latin.

'The soul is Alpha and Omega,' Peter concluded. 'What is good is what is pleasing to God.'

'Works are not good or bad in themselves,' said Simon. 'Morality is defined by men, not God.'

'Acts of charity are a guarantee of life everlasting,' said Peter. 'Miracles are proof for those who still doubt.'

'Can your God repair the damage done to a virgin?' asked Simon, glancing at his companion.

'He has spiritual power,' said Peter, visibly disconcerted by the question.

Sophia smiled an ambiguous smile.

'What I mean is, has he any physical power?' Simon went on.

'He has,' said Peter, without hesitation. 'He has cured lepers, he has . . .'

'. . . changed water into wine, et cetera, et cetera,' Simon interjected.

'Yes,' Peter continued. 'Miracles are his calling . . .'

'I thought carpentry was his calling,' said Simon.

'And charity,' said Peter.

Finally, incensed by Peter's obstinacy and constant references to His miracles, Simon said, 'I can work miracles like your Nazarene.'

'That's easily said,' Peter replied, with a quiver in his voice.

'He's picked up all kinds of tricks in the bazaars of Egypt,' said one of Peter's disciples. 'We must beware of deceit.'

'Your Nazarene – what was his name again? – he could have studied Egyptian magic, too,' said Simon.

'His miracles occurred more than once,' said Peter.

'Bury me in the earth, six cubits deep,' said Simon after brief deliberation. 'In three days I shall rise up like your . . .'

'Jesus,' said Peter. 'You know very well what His name is.'

'That's right. Him.'

One of the disciples ran off to a nearby village and returned with a group of laborers who had been building a well in the valley. They had spades, shovels, and axes slung over their shoulders. The whole village, everything that could move, came running after them. News that an Egyptian sorcerer had appeared and was going to work a miracle had spread rapidly.

'Six cubits deep,' Simon repeated.

The laborers set to work, and soon the sandy surface had been replaced by some rather coarse gravel, then by a layer of dry, reddish earth. The shovels kept turning up clay with traces of roots in it; earthworms, sliced in two by the sharp blades, wriggled and writhed in the sun as if roasting in living fire.

Sophia stood silently beside the pit, which grew deeper and deeper, while Simon – like a lord for whom a well is being dug or a foundation laid – issued orders to the men, measured off the length and breadth of the pit with careful steps, lowered his flaxen rope into its depths, and crumbled earth and sand between his fingers.

When the coffin was ready – it was made of roughly hewn boards of fragrant cypress held together by wooden studs – Sophia took off her scarf and placed it around Simon's neck. 'It's cold down there, as cold as at the bottom of a well,' she said.

Simon then abruptly left her side and took hold of the

coffin and shook it, as if wishing to test its solidity. Then he stepped in nimbly and stretched out on the bottom.

The laborers approached and, when he gave the sign, pounded the large studs into place with their broad axes. Peter whispered something to one of his disciples. The disciple went up and, having tested the studs, nodded.

Peter raised a slightly trembling arm, and the laborers slid some ropes under the coffin and lowered it carefully into the hole. Sophia stood to the side, motionless. Soil began falling on the lid; it made a noise like the beat of a large drum moving swiftly into the distance. Soon, on the spot where the hole had been, near the big olive tree, a mound resembling a sand dune took shape.

Peter climbed the mound, lifted his arms heavenwards, and started mumbling a prayer. His eyes shut, his head slightly cocked, he gave the impression of a man straining to catch far-off voices.

By the end of the day, the wind had erased all trace of bare feet and sandals from the shifting sands.

Three days later – it was a Friday – they dug up the coffin. Many more people gathered for the disinterment than had for the interment: news of the magus, fakir, conjurer had spread far and wide. As judges to whom everyone gave priority, Sophia, Peter, and his disciples stood closest to the pit.

They were struck by a revolting stench, as if from hell. Then, through the dug earth, they saw the boards of the coffin, which had darkened, as if they were rusting. The workers knocked out the studs and raised the lid. The face of Simon Magus was a mass of leprous corruption, and his eye sockets had worms peering out of them. Only his yellowish teeth remained intact, grinning as if he were convulsed or laughing.

Sophia covered her eyes with her hands and screamed. Then she turned slowly toward Peter and said in a voice that made him tremble: 'This, too, is proof of *his* teaching. Man's life is decay and perdition, and the world is in the hands of tyrants. Cursed be the greatest of all tyrants, Elohim.'

The people made way for her as she passed through their silent ranks and made for the desert, wailing.

Her mortal body returned to the brothel, while her spirit moved on to a new Illusion.